# Kids' Favorites
# Storybook Collection
## Volume 2

# Kids' Favorites
# Storybook Collection
## Volume 2

inchworm
PRESS
™

# Table of Contents

# Amanda EXPLORES THE OCEAN

written and illustrated by
**Maggie Smith**

**inchworm** PRESS ™

**New York**

Amanda Adams and her little brother Charlie were in the library. Today Amanda was reading about the ocean.

"Listen to this, Charlie," Amanda said. "'All of the oceans, including the Pacific, Atlantic, and Indian, really make up one big ocean that covers more than two-thirds of the earth.' Did you know that?"

"'At the bottom of the ocean,'" she continued, "'there are land
formations, such as mountains, valleys, and plains, just like above
the water. And there are thousands of different creatures, from
the tiniest plants and animals, called plankton, to huge whales.'"

Amanda looked at her brother. "Come with me, Charlie!
We can be fish for a day and explore the ocean . . . ."

All fish have backbones, fins, and gills for breathing. Fish use their gills to take oxygen from the water. Fish can be as small as your little toe, or much, much larger. One tuna can weigh up to fifteen-hundred pounds—that's a lot of cans of tuna fish!

Did you know that sharks are fish, too? Unlike most fish, sharks have a boneless skeleton. Their skeletons are made of cartilage—the same flexible material that is in your ears and nose. They like to eat crabs, fish, and even other sharks. Despite what you see in the movies, sharks very rarely harm people.

Not all creatures that live in the sea are fish. Some of these creatures are invertebrates—this means they don't have backbones or internal skeletons. Sea invertebrates range in size from tiny plankton to giant squid which can be  up to 65 feet long. Jellyfish, starfish, snails, and crabs are all marine invertebrates. So are sea sponges, corals, sea slugs, and marine worms. One type of marine worm is called the sea mouse—it is actually a worm covered with fur.

Sea animals can be very different from one another, but all depend upon tiny floating plants and animals called plankton. Small sea animals eat the plankton. These small animals are in turn eaten by larger animals, which are eaten by even larger animals. This is called the food chain.

Some parts of the ocean are crowded with life; others are almost barren. Most sea life is found along the continental shelf. This land begins under our feet where we first step into the ocean and stretches for miles into the sea. Sunlight can penetrate the water here and help plants to grow. Most of the seafood we eat, such as crab, lobster, flounder and cod, comes from these areas.

One of the most beautiful places that can be found along the continental shelf is the coral reef. A coral reef is a very delicate structure that is built over hundreds of years by tiny creatures called coral polyps. The coral polyps first attach to the ocean floor and then build upon each other. The corals that make up the reef are many colors and shapes. Some look like feathers, trees, or even human brains!

Many creatures live here including starfish, eels, octopi, and giant clams. There are also small, brightly colored fish, such as clown fish, angel fish, and butterfly fish. Reefs are so crowded that some species have developed ways to avoid being eaten, or even sat on. The sea urchin has dangerous spines to protect itself and is sometimes called the porcupine of the ocean.

Many large fish, marine mammals, and reptiles prefer the open seas to the crowded reef. These creatures swim far out past the continental shelf to feed and mate. Unlike fish and reptiles, mammals give birth to live young and nurse. Land mammals include rabbits, dogs, elephants, and you! Marine mammals cannot take oxygen from the water: porpoises, dolphins, and whales must come to the surface to breath. The blue whale is the largest animal on the planet, reaching more than one hundred feet long. It needs to eat two and a half tons of food every day.

Some of the world's strangest creatures live miles below the ocean surface. The sun's rays cannot reach this far into the ocean depths. These species have adapted to survive in darkness and super-cold temperatures, where there is no live plant food. Some of them catch bits of food that sink from the upper ocean. Others, such as the hatchetfish and the lanternfish, attract prey with their special lights, like fireflies do on land.

Most of the deep ocean floor is as empty as a desert, but there are some spots that are full of life. These are called hot-water vents. The heat from the vents provides a good environment for many large animals, including giant tube worms up to ten feet long and clams more than a foot wide.

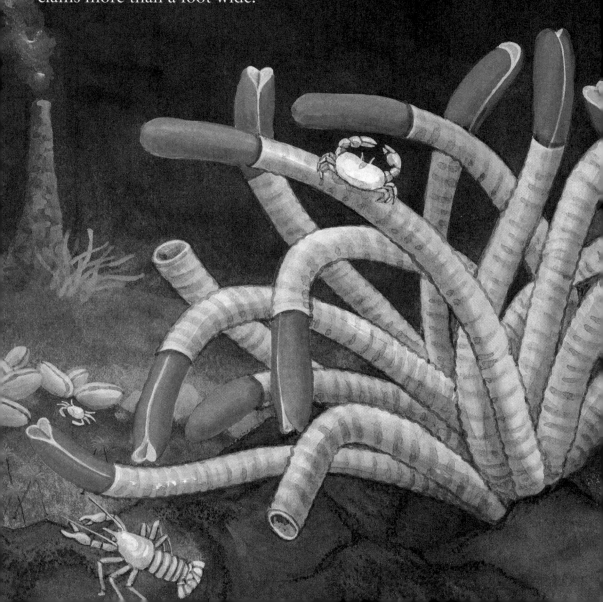

"Amanda!  Amanda!"

At first Amanda thought that a clam was calling her name, but then she realized it was her mother.

"It's time to go," said Mrs. Adams.  "Where's Charlie?"

"The last time I saw him he was swimming by a hot-water vent," said Amanda.

"Swimming by a hot-water vent?" said her mother. "Don't be silly. Oh there he is."

"Mom?" said Amanda. "I was wondering . . ."

"Yes?" said her mother.

"Well, I was just reading about life under the ocean and I've decided what I want for my next birthday present."

"What's that, my little fish?" Mrs. Adams asked.

Amanda stood up on her chair and stretched out her arms. "Scuba-diving lessons!" she announced.

# The MARTIANS NEXT DOOR

## by Ron Fontes and Justine Korman
## illustrated by Jenifer Schneider

inchworm
PRESS
TM

New York

Text copyright © 1997 Inchworm Press, a division of GT Publishing Corporation.
Illustrations copyright © 1997 Jenifer Schneider.
All rights reserved.
Designed by Lara S. Demberg.
No part of this book may be used or reproduced in any manner whatsoever
without written permission from the publisher. For information address
Inchworm Press, 16 East 40th Street, New York, New York 10016.

Zach was a curious four-year-old boy with a great imagination. He lived on a quiet street where there were no other children his age.

Then one day a new family moved in next door. Zach saw a mother, a father, and a little girl about his size. Zach heard one of the movers call the family "The Martins." He wondered what else he could find out.

The Martins looked like a normal family, except that they all wore hats.

They also had really big feet.  And their skin looked sort of greenish.  Zach had never seen anyone with green skin before, except once at the end of a roller coaster ride.

Zach ran inside. He told his parents all about the new neighbors. "They must be from Mars or something," Zach concluded.

His father laughed and said, "You have a great imagination."

His mom said, "We should be friendly to our new neighbors no matter where they come from. Why don't you go invite them to supper?"

Zach went next door. Mrs. Martin opened the door. Even though she was inside, Mrs. Martin was still wearing her hat.

Behind her, Zach saw Mr. Martin and the little girl grab their hats. But before they put them on, he saw that they had antennae growing out of their heads — just like ants! Zach was so surprised that he almost forgot to invite the Martins to supper.

Zach ran home. "Mom!" he cried. "I was right! The neighbors are Martians!"

"Are they coming to supper?" Mom asked.

"Yes," said Zach.
Zach's father didn't believe him either.
Instead, he asked Zach to set the picnic table.

Soon the Martins arrived for supper. They said their names were Dan, Ann, and Nan. They were very friendly. But they were a little strange.

Dan ate his hamburger, paper plate and all. Then he asked for a second plate.

Ann didn't know how to open a can of soda. And little Nan had a chat with the roses.

After supper, Zach asked Nan if she wanted to play catch.

"What's catch?" she asked.

So Zach taught her how to play. Then he showed her his tricycle.

"That's amazing!" Nan cried. "How does it work?"

Then the two families roasted marshmallows. The Martins liked the sticks best of all.

Zach whispered to his parents. "You see? I told you they were Martians."

But his Mom just said, "You mustn't criticize people for being different."

"But they're Martians!" Zach cried.

Then he felt someone tug his sleeve.
"Shh!" Nan whispered. "You're right," she said. "But you mustn't tell anyone or we'll have to go home."

Nan explained that her parents were scientists. They had come to Earth to learn about people. "We mean you no harm," Nan said. "In fact, we think people are great! I hope you can teach me all kinds of Earth games."

Zach laughed. "I guess it's a good thing my parents didn't believe me."

He was glad to have a friend next door — especially one who'd come all the way from Mars!

# A Child's Prayers

illustrated by *Angela Jarecki*

inchworm
PRESS

New York™

# The Lord's Prayer

Our Father, who art in heaven,
hallowed be Thy name,
Thy kingdom come,
Thy will be done,
On earth as it is in heaven.
Give us this day our daily bread,
And forgive us our trespasses
as we forgive those
who trespass against us,
and lead us not into temptation,
but deliver us from evil.
*Amen*

# Prayers for Morning

Through the night Thine angels kept
Watch around me while I slept.
Now the dark has gone away,
Lord, I thank Thee for the day.

Dear Lord, I offer thee this day
All I shall think, or do, or say.

Father in Heaven, all through the night
I have been sleeping, safe in Thy sight.
Father, I thank Thee; bless me I pray,
Bless me and keep me all through the day.

# Prayers Before Meals

For food, and all thy gifts of love,
We give thee thanks and praise.
Look down, O Father, from above
And bless us all our days.

Bless us, O Lord, and these Thy gifts
Which we are about to receive
from your bounty
Through Christ our Lord.
*Amen.*

Come, dear Lord Jesus, be our guest,
and bless what Thou hast given us.
For Jesus' sake.
*Amen*.

Thou art great
And Thou art good,
And we thank Thee
For this food.
By Thy hand
Must all be fed,
And we thank Thee
For this bread.

# Prayers for a Beautiful World

God made the world so broad and grand,
Filled with blessings from His hand.
He made the sky so high and blue,
and all the little children too.

Lord, make me an instrument of thy peace;
Where there is hatred, let me sow love;
Where there is injury, pardon;
Where there is discord, union;
Where there is doubt, faith;
Where there is despair, hope;
Where there is darkness, light;
Where there is sadness, joy.

*St. Francis of Assisi*

# Prayers of Thanks

Thank you for the world so sweet,
Thank you for the food we eat.
Thank you for the birds that sing,
Thank you, God, for everything.

Thank God for rain
and the beautiful rainbow colors
and thank God for letting children
splash in the puddles.

*A Child's Prayer, England*

Oh, the Lord is good to me,
And so I thank the Lord,
For giving me the things I need:
The sun, the rain and the appleseed:
The Lord is good to me.

*Attributed to Johnny Appleseed*
*(John Chapman — 1774-1845)*

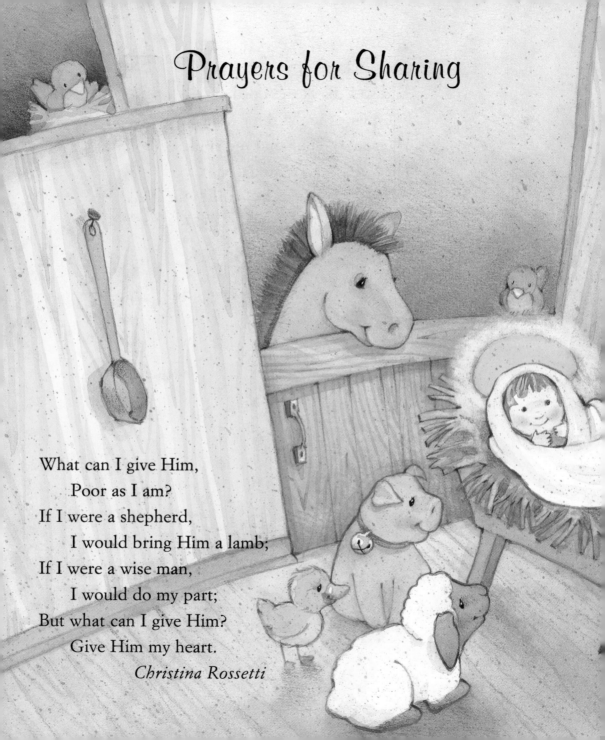

# Prayers for Sharing

What can I give Him,
  Poor as I am?
If I were a shepherd,
  I would bring Him a lamb;
If I were a wise man,
  I would do my part;
But what can I give Him?
  Give Him my heart.
    *Christina Rossetti*

God bless all those that I love;
God bless all those that love me;
God bless all those that love those that I love
And all those that love those that love me.

*New England sampler*

# Prayers for Caring

God be in my head, and in my understanding;

God be in my eyes, and in my looking;

God be in my mouth, and in my speaking;

God be in my heart, and in my thinking;

God be at my end, and in my departing.

*The Sarum Missal*

May the road rise to meet you.
May the wind be always at your back.
May the sun shine warm upon your face.
May the rains fall softly upon your fields
until we meet again.
May God hold you in the hollow of his hand.

# Prayers of Joy

All things bright and beautiful,
All creatures great and small,
All things wise and wonderful,
The Lord God made them all.

Each little flower that opens,
Each little bird that sings,
He made their glowing colors,
He made their tiny wings:

The purple-headed mountain,
The river running by,
The sunset and the morning,
That brightens up the sky,

The cold wind in the winter,
The pleasant summer sun,
The ripe fruits in the garden,
He made them every one.

*Cecil Frances Alexander*

# Prayers for Bedtime

Gentle Jesus, meek and mild,
Look upon this little child;
Pity my simplicity,
Suffer me to come to Thee.
Fain I would to Thee be brought;
Dearest God, forbid it not;
Give me, dearest God, a place
In the kingdom of Thy grace.

Lord, keep us safe this night.
Secure from all our fears.
May angels guard us while we sleep,
Till morning light appears.

# Cradle Hymn

Away in a manger, no crib for a bed,
The little Lord Jesus laid down his sweet head.
The stars in the bright sky looked down where he lay—
The little Lord Jesus asleep on the hay.
The cattle are lowing, the baby awakes,
But little Lord Jesus no crying he makes.
I love Thee, Lord Jesus! Look down from the sky,
And stay by my cradle till morning is nigh.
Be near me, Lord Jesus, I ask Thee to stay
Close by me forever, and love me, I pray.
Bless all the dear children, in Thy tender care,
And take us to heaven, to live with Thee there.

*Martin Luther*

Now I lay me down to sleep,
I pray Thee Lord, Thy child to keep:
Thy love guard me through the night
And wake me in the morning light.

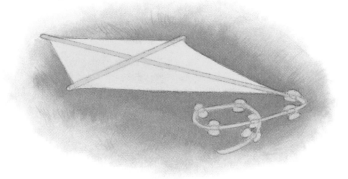

by **Cathy West**

illustrated by **Fred Marvin**

New York

"What rotten luck!" Lucky the elf said to his pet snail, Slugo.

The good luck was that it was a beautiful day. A spring wind was sweeping the clouds to the dark side of Faraway Island.

But the bad luck was that Lucky and Slugo couldn't get their kite up into the air.

"Here, Slugo," Lucky said at last. "You hold the kite like this. I'll take the string and run with it. When I say 'Let go,' you let go. Okay?"

The little snail looked worried, but he nodded.

Slugo held the kite. Lucky held the string and started to run. Suddenly a brisk wind scooped the kite up, up into the air.

"Hooray!" Lucky shouted. But he forgot to shout "Let go."
So Slugo didn't let go — he sailed into the sky with the kite.

"Don't worry," Lucky shouted to his friend. "I'll save you!"

But Lucky was nervous. And whenever Lucky got nervous,
the same thing always happened. Lucky got the hiccups.

And when he hiccuped, he accidentally let the string slip out of
his hands.  Slugo and the kite soared off into the distance — toward
the other side of Faraway Island.  The dark side.

Lucky had never been to the dark side of the island before.
But he'd heard many tales of the scary creatures who lived there.

It was the last place on earth he wanted to go.

But he knew he had to save his friend. "Slugo must be so scared," Lucky whispered to himself. He took a deep breath, hiccuped a few times, and marched off toward the dark side.

Soon Lucky came to a river. Now what was he going to do? He wasn't a very good swimmer, and the river looked awfully wide.

Just then Lucky thought he heard something.  It sounded like a giggle.  He spun around.  The bad luck was that he took a step backward and fell down the riverbank.

The good luck was that he landed on an old log and floated across the river.

On the other side of the river, Lucky hiked through the thick forest. The trail twisted and turned through the trees. At last he spotted a flash of yellow.

"Slugo!" Lucky cried. The snail and the kite dangled from a tree. Quickly Lucky helped his friend down and hugged him tight. "I'm so glad you're all right!" he said. That was the good luck.

Then Lucky looked around him. "There's only one problem," he said. "I think we're lost!" That was the bad luck. "Don't worry," Lucky told Slugo. "I'll think of something."

They sat down under the tree to think. Plunk! An acorn bopped Lucky on the head. Lucky looked up. But no one was there. Thunk! A tiny twig tapped Lucky on the shoulder. Lucky looked up again. Still he saw no one.

But then he heard something. Whispers and giggles.

Suddenly Lucky felt two "somethings" jump down on him. A pair of invisible arms wrestled him to the ground.

Poof! Two little sprites appeared out of nowhere.

"I'm Pip," said the boy.

"And I'm Squeak," said the girl.

"Follow us," Pip said. "We'll show you the way home."

"We live on the good side of the island, too," Squeak added.

Should I trust them? Lucky wondered.

He decided he really didn't have a choice. Soon it would be getting dark. And he really wanted to go home. So he started to follow them. But then —

Poof! The sprites disappeared.

"Over here!" said Pip as he reappeared beside a tree. Lucky and Slugo hurried over that way. Poof! Pip disappeared again.

"Over here!" Squeak called with a giggle from behind a big rock.

"Forget it!" Lucky said. "You'll just poof away again. Slugo and I will find our own way home."

"Wait!" Pip and Squeak cried. "We know a secret."

Lucky knew he shouldn't listen. But he stopped and turned around. "What?" he asked.

"Come on," said Pip.

"We'll show you," said Squeak.

Lucky sighed and followed them.

"Skip!" Pip ordered as they scurried down a trail.

"Hold your nose," Squeak ordered as they jumped over a log.

"Stick out your tongue," Pip commanded as they raced past a small waterfall.

"Backwards," Squeak shouted as they circled some big rocks.

Lucky was getting suspicious. He didn't think the sprites
were doing anything but fooling around. He was just about
to stop following them when they cried, "There it is!"

"It's a bridge, see?" Pip said.

"It goes to the good side," Squeak added.

Lucky grinned. "Hurry up, Slugo! We're almost home."

But just as his feet touched the bridge, Lucky heard a horrible growl.

"Who's walking on my bridge?" someone shouted. An ugly old troll crawled onto the bridge. Lucky frowned at Pip and Squeak.

"Uh-oh," Pip squeaked.

"We didn't know it was a troll bridge," Squeak said.

"See you later!" they both said. And poof — they were gone.

The good luck was that the troll said that Lucky could cross. The bad luck was that he had to pay.

"How about this kite?" Lucky said hopefully.

The troll took the yellow kite and looked at it. "Bah!" he said and threw it to the ground. "No good!"

Lucky checked his pockets. The only thing he had left was his favorite lucky penny. Sadly Lucky handed it over. The troll let him cross the bridge.

But then he stopped Slugo. "I didn't say the snail could cross," he said. "I think I'll keep him."

"Hiccup! Quick, Slugo!" Lucky cried. "Grab hold of the kite! And — hiccup! — don't let go!" Lucky grabbed the kite string and ran. Just as the troll reached out to grab Slugo, the snail and the kite flew up into the air.

The good luck was that Slugo hung on. But the bad luck was that the troll started to chase them. Lucky looked back over his shoulder. He was a pretty fast runner. But could he outrun a troll?

Suddenly he saw the troll stumble and trip. He saw the troll tumble — splash! — into the river. Bad luck for the troll. Good luck for Lucky and Slugo.

But it wasn't just good luck . . . .

Poof! It was Pip. Poof! It was Squeak. They had tripped the troll while they were invisible. They took Lucky by the hands and all of them raced away toward the good side of Faraway Island, with Slugo sailing along behind them on the kite.

When they were safe again, Lucky thanked the sprites for saving him. They just giggled. "We also picked his pocket," Pip said.

"Look," Squeak said as she held out her hand.

"My lucky penny!" Lucky cried.

The good luck was that Lucky had made two new friends. And the bad luck? Lucky couldn't think of any at all!

# by Richard Brightfield
# illustrated by Larry Daste

Ralph was playing with his dog, Peppy.

Suddenly, Ralph's mom, a volunteer rescue worker, dashed out of the house. "Just got an emergency call on my beeper," she said. "Got to run." Then, she jumped in her car and zoomed off.

Ralph heard police sirens roaring past his house.

"Bet they're headed where my mom is," Ralph said. "I wonder what's going on!"

Ralph grabbed his bicycle helmet and put it on.

"Be a good dog and stay at home with dad," Ralph told Peppy. Then he jumped on his bike and rode down the sidewalk.

Ralph pedaled as fast as he could. At the end of the block he saw his friend Sally riding toward him.

"Where are you racing to?" Sally asked.

"Did you hear those sirens? I want to find out what's happening," Ralph said.

"Do you think it's a fire?" Sally asked.

"Maybe. Want to find out?" Ralph asked.

"Sure thing!" Sally said, turning her bicycle around.
Ralph and Sally rode quickly down the sidewalk.
Suddenly, Ralph's dog, Peppy, ran up behind them.
"Peppy, go home!" Ralph shouted several times.
It was no use. Peppy continued to follow them.
"You should take Peppy home," Sally said. "He could get hurt."
"There's no time for that," Ralph said, pedaling fast.
"He'll be fine."

"Do you hear those sirens?" Sally asked. "Wait! I think they're coming this way."

"Hey, Sally, I smell smoke!" cried Ralph.

A few seconds later, a police car rushed by with its lights flashing and its siren wailing.

Just then a fire engine raced by.
"It must be a big fire," Sally said.
"Bet my mom is there," Ralph said.

Ralph and Sally followed the police car and the fire engine
Peppy scampered along behind them.
Suddenly, a large hook-and-ladder fire engine roared past.
"Wow! It must be a very big fire," Sally exclaimed.

Ralph and Sally pedaled faster down the sidewalk. Cars
were pulling over to the curb to let the emergency vehicles pass.
Just then an ambulance sped by.
"Somebody must be hurt," Ralph said.

"Look!" Sally exclaimed, pointing ahead at a huge, black column of smoke. The smoke was rising over the rooftops up to the sky.

"There's the fire!" Ralph cried.

Ralph and Sally turned the corner and saw a five-story warehouse on fire. Flames were pouring out from the windows and black smoke surrounded the roof.

They stopped a safe distance and got off their bikes. Ralph's
mom was next to an emergency van.

Peppy, excited by all the noise and activity, started running
back and forth. Suddenly, he charged, full speed toward the fire.

"Peppy, come back!" Ralph cried.

Ralph ran after Peppy, but a policeman stopped him. "You can't go any closer," the policeman said.

"But, but my dog—" Ralph stammered.

"Stay back! This is a very dangerous situation. We will find your dog, son. Don't worry," the officer said.

Up ahead, firefighters were unrolling long hoses and attaching them to a fire hydrant. Seconds later, they were spraying water on the flames.

"I'm so scared, Sally! Where's Peppy? Do you think he's OK?" asked Ralph.

"Peppy's a smart dog. I'm sure he'll be just fine."

"Help! Help me!" screamed a woman. She was leaning out a window in the burning warehouse. Thick, black smoke billowed around her.

Ralph and Sally gasped in fear. They watched as the fire-fighters put a tall ladder up against the side of the warehouse.

"You're going to be just fine. We're coming to get you now," a firefighter called up to her.

Then, another firefighter darted up the ladder.

The ladder was just high enough to reach the woman. The fireman grabbed her and carried her down to safety. The woman had fainted.

Ralph gulped and turned to Sally. "I sure hope Peppy hasn't breathed too much smoke, or he'll faint too."

"There's my mom!" Ralph cried. She was helping the woman onto a stretcher.

"Oh, no, Sally! There's no sign of Peppy anywhere and if anything happens to him it's all my fault!"

"Look Ralph! It's Peppy!" cried Sally.

Peppy was in front of the burning building, barking at the fire.

Suddenly, part of the building collapsed with a roar! Pieces of burning wood were tossed into the air. Peppy tried to run away, but a piece of burning wood fell on his tail. Yelping, he ran toward Ralph's mom.

"Oh, no! Peppy's hurt!" said Ralph weakly, trying to hold back his tears.

Ralph's mom saw Peppy coming and rushed over to pick him up. She carried him to the emergency van and put some medicine on his tail. Luckily, it was only slightly burned.

"What in heaven's name are you doing here? Did Ralph let you loose?" she said to Peppy.

Peppy looked sadly up at her.

"Is Peppy all right?" Ralph said, running up to his mom.

"Peppy is fine — now!" his mom said sternly. "What are you and Peppy doing here? A fire is no place for fun and games."

"I just wanted to—" Ralph started to say.

"We'll talk about this later," his mom said. "Right now I'm too busy." Ralph and Sally got back on their bikes and silently headed for home.

"I'm sorry," Ralph said at dinner. "I promise I'll never put Peppy in danger again. It's just that I wanted to see the rescue workers in action."

"Mom, you have an important—" Ralph started to say when the phone rang. He jumped up to answer it. "Mom there's been an accident—"

"I'm off and running," she answered, putting a last fork full of mashed potato in her mouth. Peppy barked, wagged his tail, and followed her to the door.

"Stay, Peppy," yelled Ralph. "This time we're *both* staying home!"

# LITTLE RED RIDING HOOD

by Kate Holly
illustrated by Giora Carmi

**GT**
PUBLISHING

NEW YORK

One day Little Red Riding Hood set off through the forest with a basket of food for her grandmother, who had fallen ill.

"Go straight to Grandmother's house," Little Red Riding Hood's mother told her. "And don't talk to strangers."

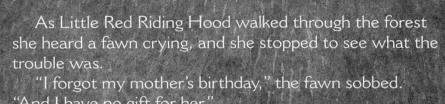

As Little Red Riding Hood walked through the forest she heard a fawn crying, and she stopped to see what the trouble was.

"I forgot my mother's birthday," the fawn sobbed. "And I have no gift for her."

Little Red Riding Hood said, "Let's pick some flowers for your mother. That would make a lovely gift."

The fawn smiled and said, "Thank you! I hope I'll be able to help *you* someday!"

As she continued her walk, Little Red Riding Hood saw a
thrush huddled on the ground. "What happened?" she asked.
"I was trying to fly, but I crashed," the thrush said sadly.
Little Red Riding Hood gently lifted the thrush and set him on
a branch. "Try again," she said gently. "I'll catch you if you fall."

The thrush was nervous, but he flapped his wings and, just like that, he was flying. The little bird was so happy that he taught Little Red Riding Hood a special tune. "Whistle just like that if you ever need me," he told her. Then he took off into the sky, whistling happily.

Little Red Riding Hood continued walking. She didn't see the big, bad wolf hiding behind a nearby tree. But the wolf saw her.

The wolf, disguised as a woodsman, stepped onto the path in front of her. "Oh, my!" cried the startled Little Red Riding Hood.

"I'm sorry," the wolf purred. "I didn't mean to scare you."

Little Red Riding Hood remembered her mother's warning. "Pardon me, sir," she said. "I must be on my way or I'll be late."

A few minutes later she stopped to drink at a stream. The wolf had followed her and was about to grab her. But suddenly, there was a loud crack, and a tree crashed down right on top of him. The wolf crawled out from underneath the tree and slunk away to lick his wounds.

The beaver who had cut down the tree waddled over to Little Red Riding Hood. "I'm sorry that tree almost hit you," he cried. "I didn't see you. We're so busy trying to build our lodge before winter."

"I'd be glad to help," Little Red Riding Hood offered.

Little Red Riding Hood fetched twigs and branches from the forest and carried them to the beavers, who built them into a sturdy lodge and dam. When they were finished, the beavers thanked her. "Call us if we can help *you* someday," they told her.

Soon Little Red Riding Hood came across an old man. She did not realize it was the wolf wearing another disguise.

When the old man told Little Red Riding Hood how hungry he was, she offered him some of the cake in her basket. He gobbled it down. Then he asked where she was going.

"My mother told me not to talk to strangers," she said.

"But we're not strangers," the wolf said. "After all, we've shared a piece of cake."

"I suppose that's true," Little Red Riding Hood said slowly. Then, not wanting to be rude, she told the old man where she was going.

The wolf said good-bye and raced down the path ahead of
Little Red Riding Hood. He reached Grandmother's house and
knocked on the door.

"Who is it?" called Grandmother from inside.

"It's Little Red Riding Hood," the wolf answered.

"Come in, dear," Grandmother said.

The wolf burst in. "Surprise!" he said with a grin, showing
his sharp white teeth. He grabbed Grandmother, shoved her
into the closet, and locked the door.

After her long walk, Little Red Riding Hood was happy to get to Grandmother's house. The windows sparkled in the sun, bright flowers bloomed along the path, and her own little swing hung from the big, shady oak tree.

When Little Red Riding Hood walked inside, the wolf was lying on the couch dressed in Grandmother's clothes.

"Good afternoon, Grandmother," said Little Red Riding Hood, and she walked over to kiss her.

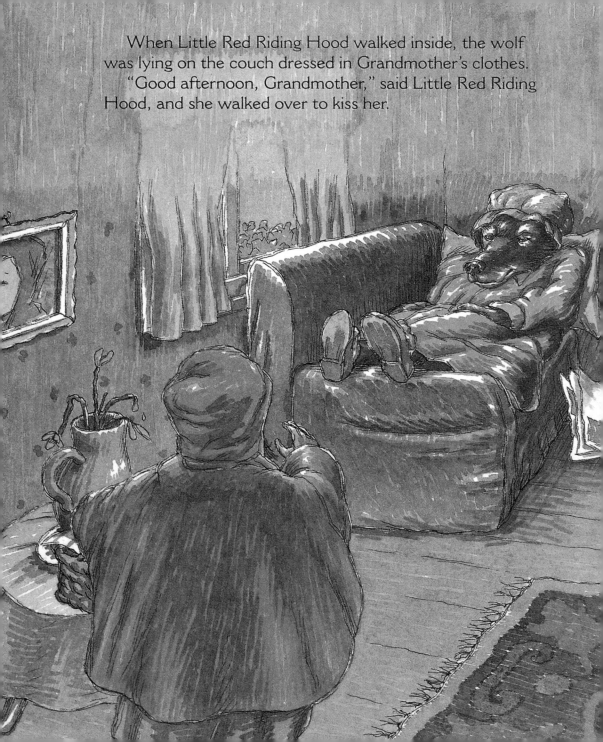

"Don't kiss me!" the wolf cried quickly, holding up his arm
to keep her away. "I -I wouldn't want you to get sick."

Little Red Riding Hood stared at the wolf's long, hairy arm
in surprise. "My, what long arms you have, Grandmother,"
she said.

"The better to hug you with, my dear," the wolf replied.
"Why don't you cut me some cake?"

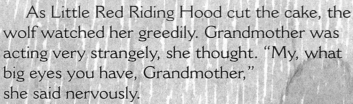

As Little Red Riding Hood cut the cake, the wolf watched her greedily. Grandmother was acting very strangely, she thought. "My, what big eyes you have, Grandmother," she said nervously.

"The better to see your pretty face, my dear," the wolf said.

Little Red Riding Hood put the cake on a plate.
The wolf licked his lips with his large red tongue.
"My, what a large mouth you have, Grandmother,"
Little Red Riding Hood said, trembling with fear.

The wolf grinned, showing his sharp teeth. "The better to
eat you with, my dear!" he cried, leaping up from the couch.
"You're not my grandmother. You're a wolf!" she cried.
She ran away, but the wolf chased after her. He was so close
that she could feel his hot breath on her neck.

Little Red Riding Hood ran and jumped on her swing. She swung higher and higher, whistling the tune the thrush had taught her.

The wolf dodged Little Red Riding Hood's swinging feet and prepared to grab her. But suddenly a flock of birds soared down out of the sky, led by the thrush. They pecked at the wolf with their sharp beaks.

The wolf fled into the woods. But Little Red Riding Hood's friend, the little fawn, was waiting with her mother. They tripped the wolf with a vine, sending him flying through the air into the stream.

The wolf splashed into the water where the beavers were waiting. They slapped the water with their large, flat tails, sending the wolf whirling around and around. Before long the stream carried him right over a waterfall and out of sight.

Little Red Riding Hood ran back inside to let her grandmother out of the closet. "I'm sorry," she said. "Mother told me not to talk to strangers, but I did. And look what happened."

"You must be more careful, dear," Grandmother said. "But thanks to your brave forest friends, there's no harm done this time."

Little Red Riding Hood's friends gathered around to watch as she hugged her grandmother for a long, long time.

# BIG BUILDERS

by **Susan Korman**

illustrated by **Joel Snyder**

Boom! Boom!
One morning a loud noise woke up Jack.
"Get up quick, Jack," cried his brother, Robbie. "There are
some big builders outside!"

Jack jumped out of bed and ran to the window.
Dozens of trees in the woods had been knocked down.
Now a yellow bulldozer was clearing away the stumps.
Jack saw some other big trucks, too.

"It's a construction site," Jack said. "Let's go see what they're building."

Jack and Robbie got dressed quickly and raced across their backyard toward the woods.

Jack liked watching the bulldozer's big caterpillar tracks roll across the ground. Its blade pushed away dirt, rocks, and trees.

"Good morning, boys!" The driver waved to Jack and Robbie. Jack waved back. "What are you building?" he called.

"Some new houses," the driver said. "Soon you'll have new neighbors."

It will be fun to have new neighbors, Jack thought.

   But he loved to play in the woods. Sometimes he and
Robbie played hide-and-seek. On other days, they found long,
pointy sticks and turned them into swords. Jack's favorite spot
was the old oak tree. Everyday he climbed the tree and looked
out at the view. Then he swung down through the branches,
just like Tarzan swinging through the jungle.

   As Jack watched the bulldozer, he felt sad. Where am I
going to play now? he wondered.

Just then Robbie waved Jack over. "Come here, Jack!" he called.

Robbie was watching the backhoe's big bucket scoop up dirt. Jack hurried over. "What's it digging?" he asked.

"A trench," someone else answered.

Surprised, Jack turned around. construction worker in a hard hat was watching the ackhoe, too.

"The backhoe's bucket digs trenches for pipes," she xplained. "Then, after the pipes are laid in the ground, the ackhoe's shovel will push the dirt back over them."

"Wow," Jack said. He didn't know that a backhoe did two jobs.

The construction worker's name was Rosa.

"It's not safe to explore a construction site without a grown-up," Rosa told them. "Would you like me to give you special tour?"

"Yes!" Jack and Robbie said at once.

Rosa went into the trailer and came out with two hard hats. "Here you go," she said, smiling.

Jack put on his hard hat. So did Robbie. Jack thought they looked like real construction workers now!

Rosa showed them a cement mixer.
Chung! Chung! Chung!
The cement mixer's barrel turned round and round.
    Rosa told Jack and Robbie that the cement mixer was mixing
concrete for the houses' foundations.
    "After the concrete is poured into the ground," she explaine
"the workers can start building the frames for the houses."

Jack noticed another truck dragging a blade along the
ground. "What does that truck do?" he asked Rosa.

"It's a grader," Rosa said. "Its job is to—"

"I know!" Robbie said. "The grader helps to build roads by making the roadbed smooth."

Rosa nodded. "That's right, Robbie," she said. Then she pointed to another truck. "Here comes the dump truck with a

load of rocks. The rocks will be used to fill in the holes before the road gets paved."

Jack watched the dump truck lift its big dumper. There was a loud noise and a cloud of dust as the rocks poured onto the ground.

The dump truck driver let Jack and Robbie climb into the cab.
He showed them how to push the lever that controlled the
dumper in the back of the truck.

After the boys jumped down from the big truck, Jack took off his hard hat and held it out to Rosa.

"Thank you for showing us all the big builders at the construction site, Rosa," he said.

"You're welcome, Jack," Rosa answered. Her brown eyes twinkled. "But our tour's not over yet. Come along with me. I want to show you one more thing."

Jack and Robbie hurried to keep up as Rosa raced across
the construction site. Where is Rosa taking us? Jack wondered

He'd thought that she'd already shown them all the big builders.
At last Rosa stopped. "Here we are," she called out.

As Jack gazed around, he felt sad again. His favorite tree was still here, but the rest of the trees in this spot had been cleared away.

"Rosa, why did you bring us here?" Robbie asked.

Rosa's smile grew wider. "I wanted to show you *your* construction site," she said.

"I don't understand, Rosa," Jack said.

"We're going to build a playground here," Rosa explained. She unfolded a big sheet of paper. "This is the blueprint for the new playground. Soon you and your family, and your neighbors, can help to build it."

"Jack! Robbie!" Their father called one morning. "Connor and Annie are here!"

Jack and Robbie put on their hard hats and raced downstairs. They were going back to the construction site with their new friends. Today was the day that they had been waiting for. They were going to build a new playground!

Jack and Connor built a jungle gym with Jack's father.
Robbie and Annie helped Rosa and Jack's mom make a fort.
Lots of neighbors pitched in to put together slides and monkey
bars, even a moving bridge!

Jack climbed up into the oak tree. He looked down at the new playground. The woods were gone, but he had helped to build a new place to play.

And it had been his idea to hang a rope swing from the oak tree's thickest branch. Now everyone in the neighborhood could swing from the tree, just like Tarzan swinging through the jungle.

Jack smiled proudly. Today he was a big builder too!

# Hera and the Hero,
# HERCULES

*by* Susan Blackaby
*Illustrated by* Mark Sparacio

**GT**
PUBLISHING
NEW YORK

Hercules. I hated him. He was a beautiful, strong baby boy. Everyone loved him, including his father, Zeus, king of all the gods and goddesses. But I, Hera, Zeus' wife and queen, wanted to see Hercules dead.

I sent two serpents to creep into Hercules' crib. When they coiled around his little tummy, Hercules woke up. He squeezed their necks until they dangled like wet noodles. I could see that getting rid of him was not going to be easy.

I was upset for years. But finally, I realized that I didn't need to kill Hercules. I could just make his life miserable. So I sent him to Tiryns to serve the foolish King Eurystheus.

King Eurystheus could not think for himself. So I made decisions for him. I had the king tell Hercules to do whatever popped into my head! And he did! First, I told him to tell Hercules to go and slay the Nemean lion. Many had tried to kill it. None had lived to tell the tale.

The Nemean lion was as big as an elephant, with very sharp claws. Hercules tracked down the lion and shot it. But the lion's hide was so tough the arrow bounced right off of it. Then the lion reared up, and Hercules grabbed its throat and dropped it at his feet. I couldn't believe my eyes.

When Eurystheus saw Hercules trudging up the road, carrying the heavy lion skin, he couldn't believe his eyes, either. His knees buckled! He was so scared that he hid in a huge vase. He sent a messenger to the city gates to meet Hercules and send him away to fight the nine-headed Hydra.

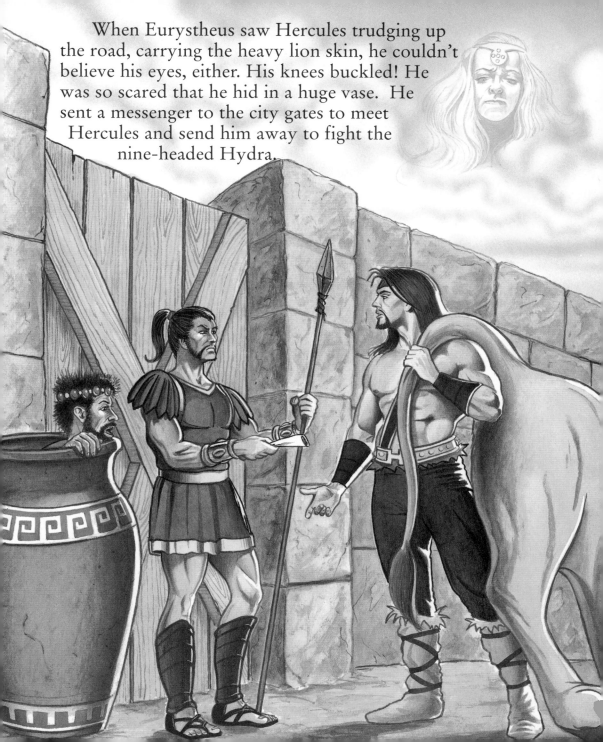

Hercules and his nephew, Iolaus, traveled together to the Hydra's swamp. The Hydra slithered toward them, tongues flicking. Hercules slashed at the creature, but each time he cut off a head, two grew in its place. I was sure Hercules was doomed. But Iolaus jumped in and burned the stumps as Hercules cut off every head.

I then had Hercules sent to trap a golden-horned doe, which was sacred to the goddess Artemis. It took a year for Hercules to find the creature. Then, as he was carrying it off, Artemis caught him. She was about to kill him, but he begged for mercy. Artemis took pity on him and let him borrow the doe to bring to the king.

Next, Hercules was told to track down the Erymanthian boar — an especially nasty, bad-tempered creature. Hercules made a terrible racket to lure the boar out of its mountain cave. Once out, the angry boar got stuck in a snow-drift and was easily snagged in Hercules' net.

King Augeus had kept 3000 cows for 30 years but had never once cleaned the stables. I gave Hercules one day to do the job. The filth and stench had driven away everyone for miles around. Rats and insects infested the place.

Somehow, Hercules managed to dam the river. Water washed over the bank, across the fields, and through the stables, leaving the countryside clean and fresh.

Next, Hercules was to slay a
flock of terrifying birds of prey.
Their feathers were steel-like arrows tha[t]
they shot at people. The goddess Athena me[t]
Hercules at the lake where the birds lived. She
gave him a sacred rattle that he could use to scar[e]
the birds. As they flapped upward, he shot
them, one by one.

What next? I was not out of ideas! I sent Hercules to capture the mad white bull that was terrorizing everyone on Crete. I was sure that Hercules would not be able to get this terrible creature to Tiryns. But with his super-human strength, he trapped the bull, dragged it onto a ship and brought it to the king.

Next, Hercules was sent north to bring back the man-eating mares that belonged to Diomedes. Many a guest had been served to this little herd. I thought they'd like a hero sandwich, but Hercules had another menu in mind. He fed Diomedes to the ponies! Then he hitched them, newly tamed, to a chariot and pranced home.

Hercules outsmarted kings and creatures, but I was certain he was no match for Hippolyte, Queen of the Amazons. I sent him to steal her golden belt, but she simply handed it to him! What was she thinking? I got the Amazons to attack Hercules' ship. He had to fight his way out, but he still managed to get that belt.

Hercules was then ordered to steal prize cattle from Geryon, the evil three-headed ogre. As usual, it took only one twang of Hercules' bow to stop Geryon in his tracks, and his little two-headed dog, too. Hercules' return to Tiryns was delayed by a gang of rustlers and one small stampede. I couldn't let him get away without stirring up a little trouble!

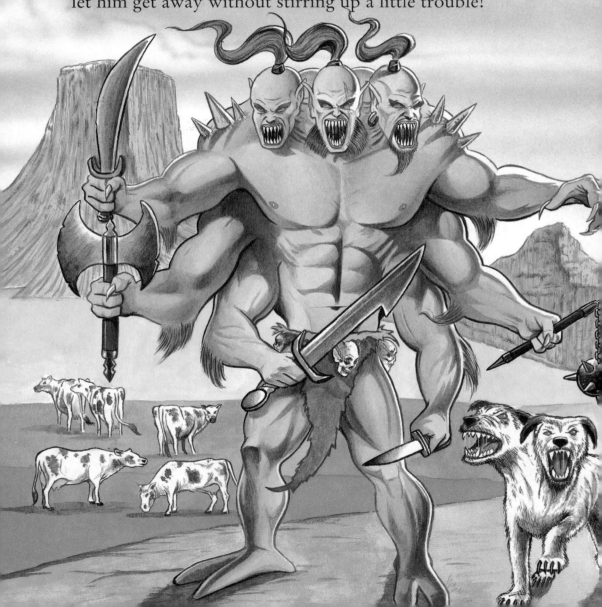

Next, Hercules was sent to a faraway town for golden apples. If the journey didn't kill him, the dragon guarding the tree would. After many trials, Hercules found the tree, the dragon, and Atlas, the giant who holds up the sky. The dragon allowed Atlas to pick the apples, so Hercules and he traded places.

While Hercules staggered under the weight of the sky, Atlas picked the apples and was about to flee. Thinking fast, Hercules convinced Atlas to hold up the sky just long enough for him to find a pad for his shoulders. Once Atlas took back the sky, Hercules grabbed the golden apples and hurried away.

Hercules' next task was to capture Cerberus, the three-headed dog who guards the entrance to the Underworld. Hades, the god of the Underworld, said that Cerberus could be taken only if no weapons were used. Hercules, with his powerful hands, carried Cerberus to the king. When Eurystheus saw them, he set Hercules free on the spot and had Cerberus returned to Hades.

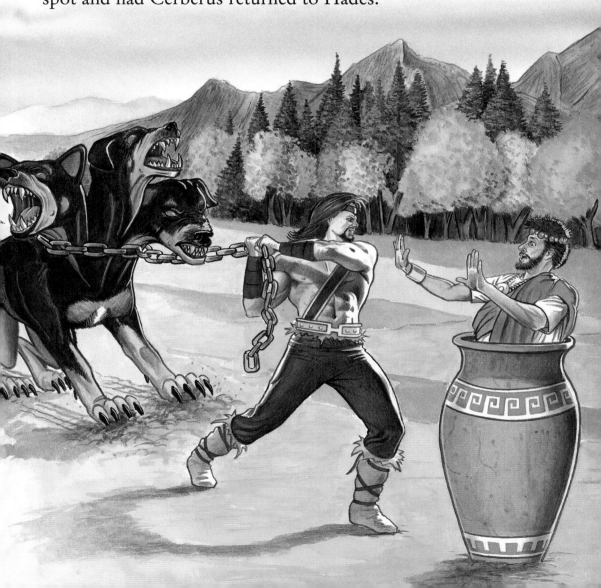

Now, I often catch sight of Hercules as he moves about the world of mortals. When his time comes, I will allow him his rightful place among the gods and heroes on Mount Olympus. Until then, when I think of it, I send along a little cloudburst just to let him know I am thinking of him.

# The
# UNICORN
# SURPRISE

by ERIC SUBEN

illustrated by CAROLYN BRACKEN

New York

Text copyright © 1998 Inchworm Press, an imprint of GT Publishing Corporation.
Illustrations copyright © 1998 Carolyn Bracken. All rights reserved.
No part of this book may be used or reproduced in any manner whatsoever
without written permission from the publisher. For information address
Inchworm Press, 16 East 40th Street, New York, New York 10016.

"Is that our new house?" cried Nina Bennett.

"It couldn't be," said her older sister, Lucy. "It looks like a castle."

"This is Greenview," said Mr. Bennett. "I'm sure we'll all love living here. Rose, the last owner, left a lot of nice old things when she moved out. I'm sure the place is full of surprises."

"Isn't the yard great?" Mrs. Bennett added. "Daddy and I are going to fix up the greenhouse for our experiments." The Bennetts were botanists, which means they work with plants.

"You two can explore wherever you want," Mrs. Bennett said. "But please stay out of the basement. The builders are coming to make Daddy and me an office down there, so it won't be safe for a few weeks."

Nina just nodded. She didn't care about the dirty old basement. "Can we go see our new rooms now?" she asked. The girls' parents had already told them that their bedrooms were in the round tower on one side of the house.

When her mother nodded, Nina raced toward the house with Lucy right behind her. Moments later the girls were climbing the tower stairs.

"Lucy, look at my room!" Nina exclaimed when they reached the second floor. She pushed aside the yellow curtains and threw open the window. "This could be Rapunzel's tower!"

"It really is like a fairy tale," said Lucy. "It even makes me miss our old house a little less. Let's go see my room!" Lucy's room was just above Nina's. It looked almost the same, except the wallpaper and curtains were blue instead of yellow. "I love it," Lucy said.

Nina looked at the staircase, which continued upward. "I wonder what's up there?"

"Probably the attic," Lucy guessed.

"Let's explore," Nina said, heading for the stairs. Lucy gulped.
Attics could be scary. But she didn't want her little sister to think
she was afraid.
"Okay," she said. "Daddy said this house is full of neat old things.
Maybe we'll find some up there."

Nina charged up the dark, winding staircase. At the top was a little door. When she pushed it open, both girls gasped in amazement. Instead of a dusty, cobwebby old attic, they saw a playroom full of treasures!

"Look at all this stuff," Lucy said.

Nina raced around the room, trying to look at everything at once. "We can play princesses up here," she said. "See? Here's a trunk full of costumes. And there's our faithful steed, on that wall hanging."

"That's called a tapestry," said Lucy. "I saw one in Mommy's art book. And that animal is called a unicorn."

"I know it's a unicorn," said Nina. "It's beautiful. Maybe Mommy will let us get one as a pet."

"Don't be silly," said Lucy. "Unicorns aren't real."

"How do you know?" Nina said, touching the tapestry. "Anyway, I wish this one was real."

"Hail, young ladies," said a deep voice.

Lucy and Nina gasped in surprise. The unicorn had stepped out of the tapestry and onto the attic floor!

Nina looked from the unicorn to the tapestry and back again. There was an empty space on the tapestry where the unicorn had been. "Are you — real?" she whispered.

"I am indeed," said the unicorn. "You wished for me, and I am here."

"My name is Lucy," said Lucy politely. "This is my sister Nina."

"How do you do. I am William," said the unicorn. "I am grateful to you for calling me from the tapestry. It has been many a year since the last young lady called me forth."

"Now that we called you, does that mean you'll play with us?" asked Nina.

The unicorn nodded and gave them a gentle smile. "What shall we do first?"

Lucy spoke up. "Our father said this old house has lots of neat surprises in it. Could you please show us some of them?"

"It would be my pleasure," William said. He led the girls to the back wall of the attic playroom. When he touched the tip of his ivory horn to one of the faded roses on the wallpaper, a panel slid back without a sound. The girls found themselves in another room full of wonderful treasures, including an enormous toy chest filled with old-fashioned toys.

In the library William showed them another secret door behind
a bookcase. When he slid it aside the girls saw a dark, twisting passageway.

"Where does that go?" Lucy asked.

"It leads to the basement," said William. "Come, I'll show you."

"Nina, we can't go down there," Lucy whispered. "Don't you
remember what Mommy said?"

Nina nodded, looking uncertain. "But Mommy didn't know about William," she said. "I'm sure we'll be safe with him. And if we don't follow William, he might not want to be our friend anymore. He'll go back into the tapestry and never come out." Lucy didn't like the thought of disobeying her mother. But suppose Nina was right? Lucy took a deep breath and stepped forward.

William led them out the other end of the secret passageway into the main room of the basement. He trotted across the wide floor to a small, arched entrance.

"This was the herb cellar," he explained. "Doesn't it smell good?"

As the girls were peering into the herb cellar, they heard foot-steps on the stairs above.

Lucy gasped. "We're not supposed to be in the basement!" she exclaimed. "If Mommy and Daddy catch us, we'll be in big trouble."

"Back to the passageway — hurry!" cried William.

The girls heard the secret door slam behind them as they raced up the stairs and through the secret passageway to the library.  They didn't stop running until they were back in the attic playroom.

"But where's William?" said Nina, looking around.

"He didn't come into the passageway with us," said Lucy. "Maybe Mommy and Daddy caught him!"

But a moment later the girls heard light hoofbeats on the stairs. "Young ladies," said a familiar deep voice. "I am here."

"Oh, William, you're safe!" Nina cried, flinging her arms around the unicorn's milky white neck. "Was that Mommy on the stairs? How did you get past her?"

"Your mother cannot see me," said William. "I can be seen only by young ladies who wish it so." The unicorn looked at the girls gravely. "Had I known that you were forbidden from exploring the basement, I would not have taken you there. You should never disobey your worthy parents."

"We know," Lucy said quietly.

"We're sorry," Nina added. "We won't do it again."

Just then the girls heard their mother calling from below. "Lucy! Nina! Dinnertime!"

"Now you must go, and so must I," said William. "Whenever you want or need me, you have but to touch the tapestry and call." Quick as a wink, he was back in his place on the wall.

"I guess Daddy was right about one thing," Lucy said, carefully stroking the unicorn on the tapestry. It felt like old dusty fabric, nothing more.

"What's that?" Nina asked, heading for the stairs.

With one last glance at William, Lucy followed her sister. "This old house sure is full of surprises!" she said.

# Humphrey
## suits
# Himself

## written and illustrated by
## Paul and alice Sharp

inchworm
PRESS
™

Humphrey felt shy about entering Ms. Ostrich's Suit Shop, but when you're an elephant it's hard to hide.

"Why, Humphrey," said Ms. Ostrich, spotting him easily, "How may I help you today?"

"My best friend Sam is having a birthday party tomorrow and I need a new suit," Humphrey said, politely.

With a leap and a twirl, Ms. Ostrich snatched up several suits. "Try these on, dear. I know you'll love them all."

Humphrey took the suits into the fitting room.

First, he tried
on the wool suit.
It was too itchy.

Next, he tried
on the plaid suit.
The colors were
too bright.

Then, he tried on the polka dot suit, but the circles made him dizzy. Humphrey decided not to try on the floral suit—it was too dainty for an elephant.

Sadly, Humphrey left the dressing room. "I'm afraid none of these suits is the one for me," he said.

Ms. Ostrich sighed. "Well, I've shown you the finest
clothes in town. You're just going to have to suit yourself."

On his way home from the clothing shop, Humphrey stopped at his friend Edward's house.

"Hello, Humphrey," said Edward. "Why are you so glum?"

"Well," Humphrey replied, "Sam's party is tomorrow and I have nothing to wear."

"Perhaps my bunnies and I can help you," said Edward, with a twinkle in his eye.

Humphrey didn't think so. Bunny clothes were much too small for him.

Edward called his children, "Victoria! Gloria! Samuel! Sylvester! Come quickly and bring Grandma's old comforter."

The four bunnies were soon quite busy. They made two armholes in a blanket and thrust it around Humphrey.

"You look. . . ," began Edward.

"Like an elephant in a bunny blanket?" said Humphrey.

". . . not quite finished," finished Edward.

"I know just what to do," said Victoria, carrying in a big, colorful box.

Humphrey could not believe it. The bunnies began to attach their Christmas decorations all over the blanket! Soon there were garlands encircling his waist and little carrot ornaments hanging from his arms. Tinsel got up his nose and made him sneeze.

"Wow!" said the bunnies, quite pleased with their work. "That's some suit."

Humphrey didn't want to hurt their feelings, but he also didn't want to wear a Christmas-blanket suit to Sam's party.

"Thank you," said Humphrey, "but I can't take all your lovely decorations from you. You've been too generous."

"Well," said Edward, "we've done all we could. You're just going to have to suit yourself."

Once home, Humphrey called his friend Sam, "I can't come to your party. I don't have anything nice enough to wear."

"Humphrey, please come," said Sam. "I don't care what you wear." But Sam also knew how shy his friend could be so he added, "Well suit yourself then."

Humphrey felt sad. He knew that Sam wanted him to come to the party. He just had to get a new suit.

Humphrey took his old suits out of the closet and lined them up on the bed.

"I  do like the pockets on my green suit," Humphrey said to himself. "I wish I hadn't lost all the buttons. The sleeves on this woolen suit are splendid. It's too bad I spilled peanut butter on the front. And this yellow jacket has great buttons, but I tore the collar when my trunk got caught in it."

Suddenly, Humphrey had an idea. He quickly gathered up scissors, pins, and thread.

The light in his room shone all that night. June bugs gathered on the window to watch Humphrey busy at work.

The next day Sam was ready for his guests. Would Humphrey
come? he wondered.

Sam's question was soon answered. There was Humphrey standing in the doorway, wearing a big smile—and a beautiful, new suit! It had green pockets, woolen sleeves, and yellow buttons. Humphrey had created a brand-new suit from his old ones.

"Happy Birthday, Sam!" said Humphrey.

"I'm glad you're here," Sam said.

Ms. Ostrich swooped through the crowd toward the two friends. "Why, Humphrey. You look fabulous," she said with a big smile. Then she said what Humphrey already knew was true, "How wonderful it is when you suit yourself!"